The Cat Who Escaped from Steerage

EVELYN WILDE MAYERSON

The Cat Who Escaped from Steerage

A BUBBEMEISER

Orlando Boston Dallas Chicago San Diego

Visit *The Learning Site!*

www.harcourtschool.com

This edition is published by special arrangement with Atheneum Books
for Young Readers, Simon & Schuster Children's Publishing Division.

Grateful acknowledgment is made to Atheneum Books for Young Readers,
Simon & Schuster Children's Publishing Division for permission to reprint
The Cat Who Escaped from Steerage by Evelyn Wilde Mayerson.

Printed in the United States of America

ISBN 0-15-314407-6

2 3 4 5 6 7 8 9 10 060 03 02 01

For Molly, Annalise, Caleb,
and anyone waiting in the wings

This story is a *bubbemeiser*—that is, a grandmother's tale. Any grandmother could have told it. There are stories like it in every family. I was just the one who wrote it down.

E. W. M.

The Cat Who Escaped from Steerage

ONE

I know none of this firsthand. The story was handed down to me the way all stories are, like a pair of earrings that a mother gives a daughter, which she in turn will give someday to her own daughter. My aunt Fruma got this story from her grandmother Feigel. Feigel got it from her brother Yonkel. And since Yonkel is the father in the story, it must be true.

The year the story took place, Halley's Comet was seen in the sky and everybody wanted to go to America. Irish, Poles, Rumanians, and Italians were running away from Europe as if from a fire. There were no airplanes; the only things in the sky were birds and an occasional dummy with no sense at all, skimming over the clouds in a hot-air balloon.

The story begins when Great-Great-Uncle Yonkel left Poland and took his family to America on a steamship. Not any ordinary steamship, mind you, but the newest model on the line with four smokestacks. It also had electricity, although not everywhere. That would have put the lamp trimmers out of their jobs. There was just enough electricity to turn the winches, pull up the anchor, power the bilge pumps, and light the chandeliers that hung in the first-class dining salon.

With Yonkel on this journey was his wife, Rifke, his daughter, Chanah, and his son, Benjamin, who later changed his name to Barton. There was also Yonkel's mother, the one my mother called Tante Mima, whose head beneath her shawl was as bald as an apple. Not to mention a cat hidden in the basket carried by Yonkel's daughter, Chanah, the nine-year-old girl who always got into trouble.

They brought with them the clothes on their backs, five dollars in gold in the heels of Yonkel's shoes, linens, four down-filled pillows, a comforter, brass candlesticks, a pot to cook in, a wooden bucket to wash in, two silver cups baked into two loaves of bread—and ten English words. Because they were so poor, they could only afford to book passage in steerage. On an ocean liner, steerage was the worst possible place to put people. It was even a poor choice for a cat hidden in a basket. Steerage was practically the bottom of the ship, directly above the cargo hold. Steerage meant nine hundred people packed together in a hold with no running water, no sink, and no windows, except for little streaked portholes that you could see through only if you stood on someone's shoulders. Steerage meant supper ladled out from huge kettles and hatch covers bolted down during storms so that the air in the hold became dank and stale.

"Whoever thought of steerage," said Uncle Yonkel, when he set his belongings on two wooden benches to mark them off for his family, "should have his tongue sewn to his nose."

"Whoever thought of steerage," said his wife, Rifke, who wiped the benches clean with a rag, "should have all his teeth pulled except one, and that one should have a toothache."

Great-Aunt Mima, Yonkel's mother, had trouble with her memory, and sometimes she chased after things she had forgotten like someone chasing the tail of a kite. If Tante Mima knew in the morning that she was in steerage, by nightfall, when everyone went out on deck to listen to the music from the first-class deck, Tante Mima would forget. "Where are we?" she would ask.

"The Taj Mahal," Yonkel would say.

This made everyone laugh because it was well known that the Taj Mahal, a palace someplace beyond Poland, was beautiful beyond belief with gold and precious jewels, and the air was as sweet as oranges. But steerage . . . well, steerage was no place to spend two weeks of your life while you crossed the Atlantic.

The children didn't mind steerage, mainly because children never seem to mind anything as much as grown-ups do. My aunt Fruma said that is because children stretch like rubber to fit any situation. The proof? Children bounce when they walk, while grown-ups walk flat-footed, like ducks.

So, while the grown-ups complained, the children made the best of it. They ran in a gang, little ones following the big ones, most wearing garlic bags around their necks to ward off fever and vampires. Few spoke each other's languages, but it did not matter. If a word was not known, a tug on a shirttail would do. They searched for land with telescopes made from rolled-up newspaper. They played tag through a deck so crowded there was no place to sit. They knocked over chessboards and got tangled in the ropes until the sailors chased them away. Sometimes they scrambled below to the baggage hold, and once, even below that, to the stokehold, where men with shovels heaped coal into fiery furnaces. Once in a while, the gang of children ducked under the chains that blocked the gangways to the upper decks, but they were usually caught and chased below by third-class passengers determined to keep steerage people where they belonged.

Wherever the children went, Chanah followed with her basket on her arm. This had been her practice ever since they boarded the ship at Marseilles, a port city in France. There, while Yonkel was arguing with the ticket agent, she had found the cat, with all her ribs showing, and had hidden her in the basket. To make room, Chanah had had to throw away her goose-down pillow, but what is a pillow when you can help out a starving, yellow-and-white-striped cat?

She named her Pitsel because she was so small. At first, Chanah managed to keep the cat a secret, especially from her father. When no one was looking, she let her out in the shadow of a gangway. She kept her basket clean and fed her scraps: a crust of bread, a piece of herring once in a while, a tiny piece of sausage left over from the Italian family on the next bench. She even tied a red ribbon on the handle of the basket to protect her cat from the evil eye, which apparently worked since Pitsel never got wild-eyed and crazy.

For a long while, the cat was undiscovered.

One reason was that steerage was noisy. So many fathers were snoring, and babies crying, and mothers arguing over who was in who's space, that an occasional meow, even in the middle of the night, went unnoticed. Even when Pitsel yowled during a storm, as the ship rolled with the giant waves, no one heard her except an Irish family who thought it was a banshee.

Chanah's first inkling that she might not be allowed to keep her cat came one sunny afternoon. Everyone was on deck jammed around the steam pipes and the ventilators. Little children sat on the shoulders of their fathers and older brothers. Someone was playing an accordion. There was no room to dance and most folks just tapped their feet in time to the music. The exception was a show-off Hungarian who attempted a wild, spinning czardas that landed him against the railing.

Chanah stood next to her brother, Benjamin, facing the ocean. She opened the basket so Pitsel could see the giant waves that washed over the bow of the ship like soapsuds. The cat apparently liked the ocean breeze, because she closed her eyes against the salt spray with a trace of a smile on her whiskered lips.

"She's happy to get away from the wharf," she said to Benjamin, "and all those rats."

As usual, Benjamin could see only the dark

side of things, like looking at the shadow and not the person. "The people on Ellis Island won't let her off the ship," he warned. "They'll send her back to France. I told you that when you first showed her to me."

Chanah had heard about the inspectors on Ellis Island. It was known that they sometimes sent people back, to say nothing of a cat. Sometimes immigrants never got to Ellis Island in the first place. She saw such a thing happen in Marseilles when the officials stopped a boy with a coughing disease from boarding the ship. His sobbing family, who didn't want to lose their passage money, had to board the ship without him while he stood on the pier with his aunt.

Chanah closed the basket shut. "They can't send her back," she whispered. "I won't let them."

Benjamin swung his eyebrows across his forehead, meaning there was no point in further discussion. Chanah put up with this kind of arrogance only because Benjamin could usually be counted on in times of trouble. In a sudden rain squall the second day on board, for example, he had yanked her into the shelter of the steerage hold. Even if he had yanked her by her braids, her safety had been uppermost in his mind.

Schmuel, on the other hand, a cousin from a neighboring village who was also on the ship, was another matter. While Schmuel was arrogant like Benjamin, he could not be counted on, certainly not for anything good. His habit ever since they had been on board was to force open the basket and thrust in his hand, then say, "Did anyone hear anything? Like a cat?"

Unlike Schmuel, his younger brother, Yaacov, brought the cat fish heads and never lifted the basket cover unless Chanah said he could. Yaacov was deaf and could speak no words. The fact was kept hidden because the immigration people on Ellis Island were also very strict about things like eyes and ears. So the story was told to everyone in steerage that Yaacov had a bad sore throat from calling geese in a windstorm and could not speak. Since his mother kept a flannel scarf dipped in turpentine wrapped around his neck, everyone believed it.

A week later, when no land was to be seen in any direction, everyone who was not seasick was outdoors listening to the music from the promenade deck. Even though they were three decks below, they could smell the Turkish cigarettes of the men and the perfume of the women and see that everything above was trimmed with brass. Chanah caught sight of a woman wearing sparkling stones on her neck and a fluffy, pale green dress, the color of a wave when it is freshly churned.

Even from so far away, it seemed to Chanah as if the woman smiled.

"Where are we?" asked Tante Mima.

"The Taj Mahal," said Benjamin. He said it like his father, and like his father, he patted the hand of his grandmother when he spoke.

Chanah thought that if the Taj Mahal was anything like the first-class deck, where passengers were given meat to eat every single day, Benjamin was not far from the truth.

It was at this point that Rifke began to have doubts about America. Even if one did not have to pay for school or became a millionaire overnight, it was clear that America was a place where men shaved their beards and women smoked cigarettes. Things were not so bad in Poland, she said. At least you knew what to expect. Yonkel disagreed. Things were terrible in Poland.

"Not so bad that a person would notice," said Rifke. They had a cellar with potatoes and a barrel full of cabbages. What else, she asked, did one need?

"Rest," replied Yonkel. "I need rest."

When the first-class passengers began to throw down pennies and candy, Yonkel decided that it was time for his family to go to bed.

They got as far as the entrance to the steerage hold, where a guard of women stood with folded arms to block the way. Only women and small babies were allowed inside. Men and older children had to wait on deck and that was that. Some of the men lit their pipes. Schmuel tried to sneak in behind his mother's trailing skirt, but the women threw him out. Even his own mother's hand was on his collar.

Rifke had a way of collecting information in bits and pieces the way a potter mends a broken pitcher. In this checkered manner, she learned that a baby was being born. She thought it was the German couple who occupied the far corner, the family whose belongings included a chair carved with lions on its arms.

By the time the baby was born, the stars in the heavens had changed places and Chanah had fallen asleep in her father's arms. She awoke for a moment to see Rifke carry a plate of soup and a red ribbon to pin to the newborn baby's woolen swaddling shawl.

That night, Chanah slept on and off, awakening to sounds in steerage, checking her basket, putting her hand inside to stroke the cat, who purred and arched her small, bony back against the lid. Chanah noticed only for a sleepy moment that the great heart of the ship never ceased its throbbing. She also noticed that the ribbon she had tied to the basket was gone.

TWO

After a breakfast of herring and potatoes, Yonkel set back his pocket watch to the time of the ship's bells. Since they were traveling westward, it was something he did every morning. Then Rifke announced that it was time to do laundry. They did the wash in a wooden bucket with a mallet to knock out the dirt and a rope to string the clothes on. Benjamin scrubbed, Tante Mima rubbed out stains, Chanah twisted the water out of everything as if she were wringing the neck of a chicken, and Rifke hung the clothes, hiding the underwear inside a pillowcase for modesty.

After the bucket and the mallet were returned to their place at the bench, Chanah rushed to pick up her basket. It felt strangely light. Chanah opened the lid slowly, so as not to frighten Pitsel. When she saw that the basket was empty, her heart felt as if it had been slammed with a wooden wash mallet. She called the cat softly. Then she began to run, darting into corners, checking beneath baskets and boxes, under benches, up high, where nets of potatoes and eggs hung in the crossbeams.

Her first suspect was her cousin Schmuel. She found him on deck watching porpoises roll beside the ship. "Where's my cat?"

"What cat?"

"You know what cat," she said.

"You mean the one you smuggled on board in the basket? Why ask me?" he said, pointing to a uniformed man with a gold braid on his hat. "Ask the captain."

The officers of the ship were mighty and unapproachable beings who strode up and down the decks like landlords' agents. Chanah knew she could not ask any of them such a question, least of all the captain, who stared down at them as if he could read their minds. Neither could she take up the matter with her mother and father. And Benjamin was of no use since all he would say was "I told you so."

Chanah would have to search the ship alone.

Where to begin on a vessel the length of her village, taller than any building she had ever seen? She was turning over this decision in her mind, the way Rifke rolled strudel dough on a tabletop, when Yaacov appeared. He came to tell her that he had a fish head for the cat. He did this by waving his hand sideways, pointing to his head, and patting his pocket. Chanah showed him the empty basket.

No talk was necessary. They took off like startled birds, sneaking through corridors, unwinding piles of rope and chain, peering down into ventilators, running through the dimly lit cargo hold past trunks and boxes piled to the ceiling rafters. When they reached the stokehold, Yaacov shook his head and fanned his face, his way of saying that the boiler room was an unlikely choice for the cat. They even scrambled beneath the canvas covers of the lifeboats. There they found oars, tins of biscuits, water casks, axes, and lockers with boxes of matches, but no cat.

They eventually reached the third-class deck after discovering that the trick was to make themselves invisible. They did this by hiding behind tea carts, behind stewards carrying trays of soup, behind wooden deck chairs where passengers lounged with their legs wrapped in blankets like sick people.

One of the passengers was Polish. The woman wasn't wearing a shawl, like Chanah's mother and grandmother, but instead, a hat with a feather. She was telling the woman beside her that she was going to live with her sister in New York and work in the garment trade. A job was waiting for her. She was to be a buttonhole maker. She would sleep on the couch in her sister's living room. But that would be only temporary. Soon she would have her own apartment.

It was the smell of Yaacov's turpentine-soaked flannel and the fish head in his pocket that made her look behind her deck chair. "What are you doing here?" she snapped. "You children don't belong here. You belong in steerage."

Chanah wondered how the lady in the feathered hat knew where they belonged, then decided to make the most of the opportunity. "Did you see anything?" she asked. She could not name exactly what she was searching for.

"What are you talking about?" asked the woman.

"Anything unusual?"

Yaacov made his hands move like cat paws.

"You two make no sense." The woman yanked her hat tighter on her head.

"Something that doesn't belong on a ship," coached Chanah.

"You don't belong on this deck," said the woman. She rang a small bell, then pulled her hat down harder, saying that she was not going to look like a greenhorn when she got off the boat.

"What does a greenhorn look like?" asked Chanah.

"They don't dress like me," replied the woman, "I can tell you." She pulled her hat to an angle. It covered an eye. Chanah figured out that if you didn't want to look like a greenhorn, you had to fix it so you couldn't see. Not out of both eyes, at any rate. The woman looked hard at Yaacov. "Why doesn't he talk?" she asked.

"He has a sore throat," said Chanah. "From yelling into the wind. After geese."

Then, before any other explanations were needed, a steward with a mustache like a brush appeared from nowhere to lead them back to steerage.

♦ ♦ ♦

The first one they saw on their return was Schmuel, who shouted that they were in trouble. Everyone was looking for them.

"We were looking for my cat," said Chanah.

"Why bother?" said Schmuel. "She's probably right this minute swimming back to France." That was ridiculous, since Schmuel knew full well that nothing alive could safely swim such a distance, not even a fish.

"It comes of going to America," said Rifke after the steward left. "It's what I was afraid of."

"Nonsense," said Yonkel. "It comes of being cooped up like a chicken."

"Thank God," said Rifke. "We thought you had gone overboard."

"Why would I do that?" asked Chanah.

"Be quiet," roared her father, who had feared the same thing. "No one has asked you anything."

The night winds began to whip the ship. It was chillier than their icehouse in Poland, where huge blocks of ice, cut by Yonkel from the frozen lake, stayed buried beneath the straw all summer. Chanah worried about Pitsel, who would surely be hungry and cold. Small wonder she hardly touched her soup, Rifke's remedy for everything.

"Where are we?" asked Tante Mima.

"The Taj Mahal, Bubbi," replied Chanah, huddled up on her section of the bench in a sorrowful ball.

Then, quite unexpectedly, Tante Mima asked, "Where is your down pillow? I stuffed it myself. It's not in your basket and it's not under your head, the only two places that it could be."

Chanah could not tell her of the third possibility: Marseilles, France. Instead, she shook her head as if she didn't know. When Tante Mima whispered the news to Rifke and Rifke, in turn, whispered it to Yonkel, they concluded that someone had stolen the pillow, most likely another family in steerage.

Yonkel spoke loud enough for everyone in the crowded hold to hear. "My daughter's pillow is missing," he said. "I don't want to accuse anybody." Of course that meant that he was accusing everybody. He said whoever did it should return it immediately, no questions asked. Otherwise, he was going to the authorities and ask for an investigation.

There was a big ruckus. Yonkel checked his shoes for the two gold pieces. Rifke pressed the loaves of bread to make sure that the silver cups were still inside. People shouted. One family dumped out all their possessions, the angry father insisting that Yonkel look for himself and stop accusing innocent people. When Rifke said she suspected the Italian family, whose leavings had fed the cat for days, Chanah confessed.

"I threw the pillow out," she said, at first so softly that she had to repeat it.

"Why? Why would you do such a thing?" asked Rifke.

She could not say that she had done it to make room for a cat. Instead, she told the first and only lie she ever told. "The basket was getting too heavy."

That made Rifke think that Chanah might be slightly crazy, like Yonkel's brother, the blacksmith, who talked to his anvil. Such things ran in families. It was best not to speak of it.

They would make do. Somehow. Tante Mima offered to take the goose down out of her own pillow and stuff two smaller pillows. This she did in a flurry of down that drifted about them like snow. That didn't solve the major problem for Chanah, which was, of course, the cat. "What about Pitsel?" she whispered to Benjamin.

"What about her?" asked Benjamin.

"She's on the ship somewhere, or else she's fallen overboard. If she's on the ship, she's probably frightened and hungry or cold, maybe even seasick. She's depending on me," said Chanah, remembering sadly how the cat had closed her eyes against the sea breeze and smiled. Chanah believed, however, that unless she got her cat back, she herself would never smile again. That night, the steward from third class, the one with the mustache that looked like a brush, feeling sorry that he had chased Chanah away that afternoon, returned with a roasted chicken wrapped in a linen napkin. But Chanah only turned away.

THREE

For two days, Chanah and Yaacov were carefully watched. No ants in any anthill were ever the objects of such close inspection. Rifke was afraid that Chanah was coming down with a fever like the old Russian uncle who lay shivering beneath a down comforter while his worried family tried to give him tea. Fevers on land were a misfortune. At sea, they were a calamity. Yaacov's mother had a different reason for keeping Yaacov close at hand. The fewer contacts he had with strangers, the less the likelihood that his deafness would be found out.

By the end of the second day, Chanah was frantic. It was bad enough losing something you had come to love. It was worse not being able to look for it. Once she thought that she heard a cat's meow. She held her breath, hoping to catch the sound again, but all she heard was the creak of the hold and the rasping breath of the old man beneath the comforter. Nothing could distract her, not even when Rifke took her to see the new baby, a tiny, wrinkled thing as red as a plum. Even when Rifke gave her the baby to hold while she smoothed the rumpled bedding beneath the mother's back, Chanah only sighed. It was the sight of the red ribbon, now pinned to the swaddling blanket, that was especially upsetting.

Naturally, Rifke felt Chanah's forehead with the back of her hand. In a time of no thermometers, it was the way you checked the temperature of a child who was behaving strangely. Rifke was distracted, however, by the wailing Russian family. When the sick man refused to take even tea, all agreed it was a very bad omen. No one was surprised when the officials were summoned. Nor were they surprised when minutes later the old man was carried away on a stretcher. Benjamin learned that he was being taken to some sort of a sick house called the *infirmary*, which, of course, became the family's eleventh English word.

"A terrible thing," said Rifke. "That's what comes of running wild."

Chanah had never seen the old Russian uncle walk, much less run, but she had learned that in moments like these, it was better not to argue.

As if things weren't bad enough, it began to rain. The harder the drops, the more crowded grew the steerage hold. Soon it was more jammed than at night, when there were always some people out on deck staring at the stars. Yonkel said that when the weather was good, they were like potatoes in a barrel, but when it rained, they became sardines in a tin.

Soon the wind was up, as if wound by a giant hand. It howled down the steps and skimmed the corners of the steerage hold. Those lucky enough to have shawls wrapped them over their faces. When the ship began to pitch and roll, sailors rushed to drive those remaining on deck down the slippery stairs. These passengers did not go willingly. They preferred the rain to hatch covers shut tightly over their heads.

Lanterns swung in the gloomy beams. The air became muggy and humid, making the hold like a steam bath without towels. Someone began to play a harmonica. Despite its cheerful sound, passengers became restless. They thrashed and fidgeted, fighting for space to stretch out a leg, room to lay down a bedroll, a whiff of air that was not foul. Some who had not been seasick before were seasick now. Ordinary conversations turned into quarrels.

"We're going to Philadelphia," one man announced in a loud, cranky voice.

"What is Philadelphia?" challenged another.

When the first man replied, "A town like New York," a third voice shouted from nowhere, "Philadelphia is no more like New York than Minsk is like Pinsk! Take it from one who knows!"

It was at this point in the voyage that they began to complain about their water. Left for them daily in casks, it had begun to taste bitter and rancid, and there was never quite enough. To drink, maybe, but not enough to wash in or, if a man was so inclined, to shave. Each day's ration seemed to be less than that of the day before. Someone suggested that charcoal would make the water taste better. When another recommended vinegar, Chanah fell asleep.

That night, she awoke to a crashing slam and a great jolt, which knocked her off the bench. When she tried to stand, water rolled in over her ankles. People began to scream. Sailors wearing rain gear came rushing down into the hold with water pumps and buckets. Certain that the ship was going under, some passengers took out crosses and rosary beads, while others put on prayer shawls and wrapped their arms with leather straps called tefillin.

Yonkel had no such conviction. He was going to be a farmer in New Jersey and believed that one was expected to cooperate in one's safety. "My family," he shouted, "is not going to drown! Not if I can help it!" He turned their benches upside down and, with Benjamin's help, tied everyone in with ropes. He did the same for Yaacov, Schmuel, and their mother, Raizel, traveling without a man because her husband, Shimson, was already in America. If the ship sank, they, at least, would float.

The ship didn't sink but instead rolled, then slammed, rolled again, staggered, heaved, and slammed again while Rifke said that if she could only jump overboard, she would swim back to Poland and never complain again. Chanah began to cry, certain that her cat had been sent flying into the water.

In all this turmoil, Tante Mima suddenly seemed to know where she was. "Don't tell me that this is the Taj Mahal where my granddaughter is crying her eyes out," she said. "Stupid I'm not."

By the next morning, the sound of the wild, driving rain had stopped. The pitching of the ship had turned into gentle dips, like the rocking of a cradle. The hatch covers were opened, and cool, clean air fluttered in like ribbons. Everything had to be hauled outside to dry—boxes, pillows, comforters, afghans, overcoats, shoes, carpetbags, parcels wrapped in string, even the wooden chair carved with lions on its arms. It was during the drying-out period, when Rifke and Yonkel were organizing their soggy belongings on the teeming deck, that Chanah had another chance to search the ship.

It was easy to slip away. Volunteers were sweeping the deck and throwing the garbage into the sea. Waiting on the crest of a wave were petrels, sea fowl with black and white plumage, who dipped down into the trough of the wave, only to rise again on a new pinnacle. As the petrels flew to the garbage and the buglers on the decks above announced the midday meal, Chanah ran. Yaacov was right behind her, as close and as silent as a shadow.

When they were safely behind a funnel, she pointed to her ear to tell him that she had heard a cat. Pitsel had to be someplace near. But not in steerage, where someone would have noticed her. That left the cargo hold. They slipped below to search again.

Water on the wooden floor of the cargo hold

sloshed beneath their feet. Chanah tried not to be afraid as they trudged through narrow aisles piled to the ceiling. She told herself that the forests in Poland were far more dangerous. There, wolves hid behind the trunks of trees, and dybbuks, waiting for the right soul to steal, nestled in the forks. What surrounded them here was only baggage.

Suddenly Yaacov lifted his head, then turned and began to climb the mountain of luggage hand-over-hand, pulling up Chanah behind him.

"Where are we going?" she asked.

He pointed toward a specific spot, the top of a double hatbox on top of a trunk.

There they found the small bones of a mouse picked as clean and as shiny as a whistle, and nearby, yellow and white hairs. The cat had been there. There was no doubt. But where had she gone? They scrambled down and ran through the aisles of the cargo hold until Chanah heard footsteps and they were forced to duck behind a steamer trunk.

Two crewmen wearing starched white jackets as shiny as cake pans were checking luggage tags. They seemed to find what they were looking for—a set of leather bags, which they lifted onto their shoulders and carried away.

The crewmen disappeared into a narrow hatchway. Chanah and Yaacov followed. In the hatchway was a steep ladder that led upward. For Chanah it was no different from climbing the ladder that led from the hearth in Poland to her sleeping loft, except that this ladder seemed to go on forever.

Their sodden shoes squeaked from rung to rung as they discovered that the trick was not to look down. Suddenly, the ladder began to clang below them. Someone was climbing up. Chanah heard it. Yaacov felt it in the vibrations in his hands. They scurried to a level place, then ran through an exit onto a deck with lifeboats hoisted high overhead.

Along the deck were white-uniformed ship's officers and passengers in straw hats looking out to sea. Chanah and Yaacov peered over the rail to see how high they had gone. They located the steerage deck below, where a crowd of passengers were spreading their belongings in the sun. Everyone looked small, like dolls made of clothespins.

A ship's officer looked at them keenly before he turned to offer a salute to a lady with a parasol. Chanah sized up the situation and pulled Yaacov behind a giant spool of chain. She was determined that they would not be sent back because they looked like greenhorns. It had something to do with headgear.

"Don't run," she said. "Walk slowly, as if you

belonged here." She whipped off his cap. "I don't see anyone wearing anything like this. It's all wet, anyway." Then she untied her kerchief and stuffed it into a pocket of her pinafore.

It wasn't easy to act as if they belonged. Surprises everywhere made them stare in wonder, such as floor-to-ceiling mirrors, doorways with portieres of crimson velvet, music rooms with draped pianos, floors made of tiny bits of marble, even a sweet-smelling flower shop, where a man was having a carnation pinned to his lapel.

When it looked as if the ship's officer had begun to follow them, Chanah and Yaacov sprinted back to the funnel hatch and climbed as fast as they could to the next deck. There, stopping only to catch their breath, they saw that this deck was more open than the ones below. Except for low buildings in the center, it was as clear as a farmer's field. One could see all the way to the other end, where passengers in white whacked a rubber ring back and forth across a net. High above the net, a sailor sat in the crow's nest looking out to sea.

Chanah heard dogs barking. She couldn't tell where the sound came from. She told this to Yaacov, adding that where there were dogs barking, there might be a cat. He circled the air with his finger to ask where the sound was coming from.

She shook her head to tell him that she didn't know.

Two ship's officers were coming their way, looking angry. They marched in quickstep. Chanah and Yaacov ducked behind a ventilator and sought a funnel hatchway, where they scurried down, down to what they thought was the bottom. When they stepped out, they saw that they had made a mistake. They had not reached the gloomy cargo hold but the sunlit third-class deck. There, as if waiting for them, stood the steward with the mustache that looked like a brush.

Instead of leading them by the necks to the hold below, as someone else might have done, he asked them gently what they were doing out of steerage.

Chanah tried to change the subject, a skill she would come to master later in life. She asked him if there were dogs on board.

He replied with some pride that this ship had everything, even kennels in which passengers could keep their pets. "You like dogs?" he asked.

"Yes," she replied, which wasn't exactly true, yet neither was it untrue, since she had never actually known a dog.

"I'll show you how to find the dogs, but don't say who told you."

Chanah promised him that they wouldn't. The

steward took out a luncheon menu and a pencil, and on the back of the menu drew a map of the ship, including the wheelhouse high above, where the officers watched the ocean and took their sightings of the stars.

Just below the wheelhouse, on the deck above the net-and-rubber-ring game he called tennis, were the kennels. But they were tricky to get to because one could be seen from the wheelhouse. Also, one could be seen by passengers who sometimes came to take their dogs out or to play with them through the wire mesh.

Then, with a quick glance over his shoulder, he told Chanah and Yaacov to get below before it was discovered that he had not reported them, much less given them a map of the ship.

On their way, Chanah noticed the Polish woman standing against the railing looking sad and wistful, the way lonely people sometimes do. Chanah dipped her hand into her pinafore pocket and brought out her softest down feather. "I have something for you," she said.

"What do I want with this thing?" asked the woman, looking about to see if anyone noticed that she was talking to children from steerage.

"You can put it on your hat," suggested Chanah.

"You little bumpkin. I would never put this on

a hat." Then the woman held the feather over the rail as if to let it drift into the wind.

♦ ♦ ♦

When they returned to steerage, no one seemed to know that they had left—except Schmuel. "Where were you?" he asked. "Looking for that stupid cat, I bet. The old man that they took away on a stretcher has a better chance of coming back than that cat." Schmuel turned to his younger brother. "And why is your cap off your head?"

Yaacov told him through a series of signs that he was drying it in the sun.

"I don't believe you," said Schmuel. "You probably lost it."

Yaacov put up both palms and shrugged his shoulders to say "I can't help what you believe."

That evening, in the corner of the hold, a small huddle of men were making plans to raid the third-class supply room for fresh drinking water. Sometimes, they argued, it was necessary to take matters into one's own hands. Yonkel was against it, even though there seemed to be a shortage. Stealing was stealing, even if it was only water. The water in steerage wasn't the best, he agreed; at worst it was like a sour well. But they had enough for their needs and soon they would be in

America, where they would have all the water they wanted. One only needed patience.

While everyone in steerage waited to see what the outcome of the argument would be, Schmuel whispered something to his mother, and Chanah and Yaacov studied the map to figure out how to get to the kennels.

Their investigation was interrupted by Yaacov's mother, standing before him with her hands on her hips. "Your brother says you lost your cap. What do you have to say for yourself?"

Yaacov pulled his cap from his pants pocket and waved it in the air like a flag. Satisfied, his mother lifted her long skirt and took off after his older brother, warning for all to hear that someone was going to get it.

Small wonder that with all this attention elsewhere, the first ones to notice the captain standing in the doorway, with an officer on either side, was the Russian family, certain that he came to bring bad news.

FOUR

At the sight of the captain and his splendid officers, all whispering stopped as if someone had caught it in a bag. The Russian family, waiting for news of their uncle, stood with their hands to their throats. Women clutched their shawls and their children. Men stood and brushed back the hair on their heads with the palms of their hands. Those in the huddle continued to plan their water raid for only the time it takes to lace up a shoe. Then, slowly, one after another turned to find the captain standing solemnly in a uniform without a crease with four rows of gold-wire stripes on his sleeves. On either side of the captain stood an officer, one with a pair of binoculars around his neck, the other holding a burlap bag.

To everyone's surprise, the captain smiled. "I understand that a baby has been born," he said.

The unofficial translators interpreted his words into many languages. When it was known why he had come to the steerage hold, everyone breathed a sigh of relief, including Chanah. She was certain that they had learned about her and Yaacov scavenging the ship and had come to take them away. The Russian family dabbed at their eyes.

"May I see the child?" the captain asked.

The German father proudly led the captain and his party to the makeshift cradle. There the baby lay, wrapped tightly in a swaddling shawl. In those days people thought it was harmful for an infant to kick and move its arms, so babies were bandaged in their clothes. If it is a thing of wonder today when a baby learns to walk, at that time it was a miracle.

The captain turned to the parents. "I have the authority to christen the baby," he said. "That is, if it is your wish that I do so."

Again the translators translated. Everyone gasped and nodded to one another. Even if it was not one's practice to christen one's babies, it was clear that this was a great honor. When the mother and father nodded in agreement, the captain presented the mother with a small carton of eggs. Then he closed the baby's fingers around a pinch of salt in one tiny fist and a coin in the other, sprinkled the baby with seawater, and gave her a name, which changed in the retelling from Ermintrude to Rita.

One of the officers opened the burlap bag. The captain dipped in his hand and brought out a fistful of sand, which he spread beneath the baby's feet.

Seeing the puzzled look on everyone's face, he quickly explained that on a ship sand was stored for ballast in the bilge. The translators shouted their translations over the heads of the mob. "Since this sand comes from Staten Island," the captain announced, "this little one is the first among you to set foot on American soil."

Everyone cheered. It is said that even the lanterns spun. Those who knew explained where Staten Island was. One had it on the western shore of Nova Scotia. Another placed it in California on the coast facing China, which didn't sound right to anyone with a sense of location. It didn't matter. All the steerage passengers, including the Russian family, were caught up in the joy of the moment.

◆ ◆ ◆

When everyone crowded around the cradle, Chanah ran out of the hold to the funnel hatch. There, in a shaft of sunlight and huddled out of sight, she and Yaacov unfolded the menu and studied the penciled map.

Yaacov put his finger on the *X* that marked the location of the kennels and Chanah nodded. It was where they would most likely find Pitsel. The reason was simple: If her French cat was like Polish cats, she would enjoy tormenting tied-up dogs by sitting out of reach and cleaning her whiskers.

Chanah and Yaacov were so wrapped up in the map and in the selection of a passageway, they didn't notice Schmuel sneak up behind them until he poked them in the ribs. He insisted on going with them. He had no interest in the cat, only in showing that he could go where he pleased, as if he, like the captain, wore gold stripes on his sleeves. Since he was older, they had no choice but to let him come along.

Staggering with the motion of the high rolling seas, the three finally reached the top deck with its four towering smokestacks higher than any silo, and a bridge where suntanned officers of the watch navigated the ship.

Chanah shaded her eyes to scan the deck. At the rear she found what they were looking for, a small building circled with a fenced run in which dogs scampered round and round as if they were really going somewhere.

Scurrying from one ventilator to another, the children zigzagged toward the kennel, ducking into a shadow when they noticed sailors on a rigging painting a smokestack. There, under cover of the shade, they took up watch positions, Chanah on her belly, Yaacov with the penciled map rolled into a telescope, Schmuel twisting his lips into a prune.

"What do you expect to see?" asked Schmuel.

"My cat," replied Chanah, on her elbows, her chin supported with her hands.

"You simpleton, there's no cat here," said Schmuel. "Although there might have been one once," he added with a wicked smile.

Yaacov pointed to a woman who stepped on deck with a dog on a red leather leash. The woman swayed against the railing, then handed the leash to a crewman as another crewman emptied a sack into a feeding trough.

While Chanah and Yaacov waited as still and as motionless as the shadow in which they hid, Schmuel became restless. "I'm hungry," he said. Then a moment later, "It's hot up here." And a moment after that, "I'm thirsty."

Yaacov signaled that he knew where there was food and water. He made a giant circle with his arms. *All a person could want.* He slipped one hand beneath another. *Beneath the canvas covers of the lifeboats.*

While Yaacov made the hand signs for twisting open a tin and turning on a spigot, Chanah saw a sudden, quick motion. She caught her breath in her throat and held it. What was at first a blur took the form of a cat, creeping on light, quiet paws from behind a ventilator.

Pitsel stopped her stalking, lifted her ears, and turned, then looked at Chanah. She appeared scruffy and underfed, the skin of her flanks flapping like sails.

"It's me, Pitsel," called Chanah as loudly as she dared, "Chanah with the basket! Chanah who gave you sausage and pickled herring!"

The cat switched her tail in a lofty, elegant wave, then stepped daintily in the direction of the waiting children. Just as she was close enough to touch, Schmuel jumped up and Pitsel took off with a yowl. Chanah fled after her with Yaacov on her heels and Schmuel behind them, huffing and puffing, shouting for them to stop.

They followed the cat down to the next level, past wireless rooms where radio operators were tapping messages across the Atlantic, then chased her down to the third deck where brightly painted wooden racehorses stood on chalk-marked squares. The children chased Pitsel past a man rolling dice and bumped into stewards moving the horses forward.

"A cat!" shouted the Polish woman, who now had a new down feather tucked into her hat.

"Three children from steerage," shouted the man rolling the dice.

"My horse," yelled a man in knickers. "They've knocked him into the wrong square!"

Chanah almost caught her cat. She actually felt the soft fur of Pitsel's back when two ship's officers came out of nowhere to block her path. Schmuel, who must have seen the officers coming, turned and ran in the other direction, but Yaacov, loyal cousin that he was, stood bravely at Chanah's side.

"Stop right there," commanded an officer. "What are you doing out of steerage?" he asked in their language.

"We wanted to see the ship," replied Chanah, providing, if not the main reason, nonetheless, a reason.

"Is that true?" asked the officer of Yaacov. "Is that why you climbed to the bridge deck? Or are you looking for mischief?"

Yaacov looked puzzled.

"Why doesn't he talk?" asked the other officer.

"He has a sore throat," replied Chanah.

Just then, a clanging ship's bell signaled the hour. Chanah clapped her hands to her ears, as did the officers. Only Yaacov stood patiently waiting, his hands at his sides.

One of the officers frowned as if trying to figure something out, then walked behind Yaacov and suddenly clapped his hands.

Again, Yaacov simply stood waiting.

"He's stone-deaf," said the officer to the other. "Make a note for the fellows at Ellis Island."

Chanah and Yaacov were escorted back to steerage with firm hands on each of their shoulders.

They were making their way down the last steps when they came upon the men who had been plotting to steal water from third class. Huddled against the railing with tins in their hands, the group seemed as startled to see Chanah and Yaacov in the custody of the officers as the officers were to see them.

"What are you men doing on the third-class gangway?" demanded an officer.

Yonkel was the first to speak. "We were looking for my daughter and my nephew," he replied. "Thank God they're found." He lifted Chanah in one arm and put his other arm around Yaacov.

"This is very serious," warned the other officer. "You people from steerage must stay in steerage. You do not have the run of the ship. If it happens again, then we will have no choice but to turn those who do not follow rules over to immigration."

"It will not happen again," promised Yonkel, as the mob broke up and scattered the way oil beads up on water.

To Chanah's surprise, her father was not angry, not even when she told him that the reason they had been on the upper decks was to search for a cat that she had kept hidden in her basket. He told her that she had saved him from doing something he would have been ashamed of. She was not sure how she had done this, but she didn't argue.

Later, after Schmuel was brought back, caught with tins of biscuits hidden under his shirt, no one was surprised when crewmen were posted at the gangways to ensure that those from steerage stayed where they belonged.

Sadness, like fish, was swallowed up by greater sadness. Later that day the old Russian uncle died. Out of respect, everyone who could went out on deck to watch the burial at sea. When Chanah cried, it was not for the body wrapped in a shroud that slid beneath the waves. It was for the cat that she would certainly never see again and for her cousin Yaacov whose deafness had been discovered.

She did not mention the business about the note until later that night when the wailing of the Russian family filled the steerage hold and one could do nothing but think. After Yonkel told Yaacov's mother, she, too, began to cry, making the night a long, sad affair that seemed as endless as the ocean.

FIVE

Even before Rifke took Chanah out on the open deck to wash her hair and dry it in the sun beneath squadrons of screeching sea gulls that whooped overhead, Chanah knew that this day was different. For one thing, the slamming wind that had sucked the breath from their throats had changed into a light, steady breeze. For another, the sea that surrounded them as far as the eye could see had changed. Where before the ship had plunged to meet the mountainous waves head-on, now it cut through ridges of water that lapped over other ridges, each scurrying over another in a rush to climb to a lofty top that foamed like soap.

The last thing she noticed was that instead of an occasional distant sighting of another ship, now there were a half dozen vessels close enough for one to see their markings.

Rifke was uninterested in Chanah's observation. Certain that Chanah had caught ringworm from the cat, her main interest was health, and she continued to comb kerosene through Chanah's scalp before braiding her hair. When Chanah complained about the smell, Rifke was unsympathetic.

"No one asked you to pick up a dirty cat," she replied.

Yaacov watched in the shadows, waiting for Rifke to tie the ends of Chanah's braids and join the other women. Then he pushed through the crowded deck to tug at Chanah's skirt.

"My cat?" she whispered hopefully. "Did you see her?"

Yaacov shook his head. *No cat*. Instead, he sliced through the air, making a flat, sweeping path with the edge of his hand. *Land,* he said.

Chanah leaned over the railing and peered out as far as she could, squinting over the cloud of foam and spray that tossed from the bow of the ship. "Where? I don't see anything."

Yaacov shook his head. *Land,* he insisted, pointing to some distant horizon, until his mother, fearful that he had attracted enough attention for one voyage, came to yank him back to the cover of the steerage hold.

Later that evening, when speculation ran like a mouse from one end of the steerage hold to another, Yonkel made an announcement to his family. "We're getting close to America," he whispered, as if the idea were his alone. "Very close." That led to a detailed discussion of who was to carry what, with strict instructions to keep as tight as grapes.

Chanah had seen grapes only once. "How tight is that?" she asked. "I forget."

Yonkel turned to Rifke and jerked his chin toward Chanah. "Keep an eye on that one," he said.

Chanah refused to carry her basket, now woven with too many sad memories. Rifke protested that it was time she was reasonable since reason was one of the things one was tested for. "How are you going to get into America," she asked, "if you're not sensible?"

"She depended on me," was all Chanah could say. She didn't care if the Americans thought she had sense or not.

Tante Mima solved the problem by offering to carry the basket herself along with the two rock-hard loaves of bread in which the silver cups were safely tucked.

After Yonkel instructed Benjamin to keep an especially watchful eye on his grandmother, Yonkel and Rifke went to talk to Yaacov's mother, who had become more worried with each tolling ship's bell. Yonkel told her that there was a good chance that the officer's note about Yaacov's deafness would somehow get lost. There were too many immigrants to process—almost nine hundred from steerage and three hundred in third class alone. Besides, why would the authorities be interested in one small boy? Rifke said that if worse came to worst, they would insist on the original story, that Yaacov had become hoarse from calling geese. How could the immigration officials dispute such an obvious explanation?

♦ ♦ ♦

The next morning they awoke to an awful din. Eager to find out what all the commotion was about, Chanah's family ran out on deck in an awkward cluster, banging into other people, even knocking over a cooking pot and a checkerboard. Each one holding the hand of another, they quickly saw that everything was veiled in an early-morning mist as dense as steam from a kettle.

They were in a bay, surrounded with islands and fields, hills and woods, and rivers that poked into the bay like watery fingers. About them in every direction were tugboats, barges, sailboats, freighters, and ocean liners moving like slugs, all blowing whistles and horns or clanging bells.

The mist cleared slowly as the sun rose, revealing the shapes of tall buildings of the city beyond. The buildings were higher than any they had ever seen in Poland, including a church with a steeple and a turreted castle that had cast the entire village in shadow.

Then something wondrous appeared. To their left, rising before them, stood a giant statue of a woman holding aloft a torch in one hand and clutching a book in the other. Rays like the spokes on a wheel poked from her head.

Tante Mima tried to cover Chanah's eyes. "Don't look," she said. "She's in her nightgown."

"If the Americans want to put the Statue of Liberty in a nightdress," said Yonkel, "it's their business."

Everyone in steerage began to shout at the same moment. Some began to cry. Parents picked up babies and small children and held them up to see the lady with the torch. Chanah felt as if the lady was looking right at her. She did not really believe it, but it was nice to pretend until Benjamin spoiled it by saying that she was only made of copper.

Things happened quickly after that. A booming gun salute was fired from an island to their right. Crewmen ran shouting among the passengers in the steerage hold with orders for everyone to wear their tickets in plain sight, the men to fasten them to their caps, the women to their dresses. Then, carrying bills of lading in their trembling hands, the steerage passengers gathered on deck with their bundles, trunks, boxes, baskets, while the passengers on the upper decks threw down coins or waved to people waiting on the wharf.

"Don't pick up their pennies," warned Yonkel. "Soon we will be richer than rich."

"I," said Rifke, "will settle for a roof over my head and a floor that doesn't rock."

They were poked and shoved into a long line that led down the gangplank, where they were herded into waiting ferries. At this moment, Yaacov's mother thought she saw her husband, Shimson, waiting on the wharf. She began to wave to a man who waved back, but before she could be certain, she was rudely shoved along with everyone else into a ferry.

"Wave to your father, Schmuel," she shouted.

"Where?" asked Schmuel. "I don't see him."

"Why do you tell them that that man is Shimson," asked Rifke, "when you are not sure? When you cannot even see his face?"

"It will help to have something good to think about," replied Yaacov's mother, "while we wait in that place." She pointed in the direction of Ellis Island, to which they were headed.

Chanah paid attention to none of this. She was taking one last look at the ship that had been her home for the last two weeks. If there was any hope of ever seeing Pitsel again, it would be gone the minute she stepped foot on the ferry. Her deep sigh went unheard when passengers suddenly began to tug and shout as their baggage was torn from them and thrown into the ferry's lower deck. Most had not been separated from their possessions since they had left their homes, and having their personal belongings yanked from their hands was an unsettling experience.

For Chanah's family it was less so, mainly because they had so little of value. Whatever was important, like the silver cups, the brass candlesticks, and the gold coins, was carried on their persons.

Chanah wondered about the woman from third class. Did she have to go to Ellis Island? Did they tug the luggage from her hands, too?

"Where are we going now?" asked Tante Mima. "Are they sending us back already?"

"Not back, Mama," replied Yonkel. "Just to Ellis Island."

"What for?" asked Tante Mima.

"To look us over. To make sure that we're fit to enter." He said this softly, so that Yaacov's mother wouldn't have more to worry about than she already had.

SIX

The ferry ride to Ellis Island was brief, only fifteen minutes by Yonkel's pocket watch, the time it takes to pluck a chicken, pinfeathers and all. As Chanah and her family stepped on the dock, they were surrounded by guards who looked as if they did not know how to smile, all scowling and gesturing, shouting commands, pulling the immigrants into separate groups, then counting them and shoving them into line when they did not move quickly enough.

Chanah and her family were pushed into a redbrick building, where they climbed a staircase, lugging their bundles and their baskets one step at a time. At the top of the staircase they were stopped by a team of doctors in long gray coats who inspected their faces, hair, necks, and hands, with careful attention to their eyes, then listened to their hearts. Others did not pass inspection and were taken out of line, including the Russian family, who were all being detained to determine if they were carrying disease.

When the doctors finally waved them through, Chanah and her family stepped down another flight of stairs into a great hall. Yaacov, Schmuel, and Raizel were right behind them. The conclusion that none of them dared make was that the note from the ship's officer had somehow been lost.

The great hall below was divided into a maze of passageways for the immigrants to pass through, clearance lines bound by iron pipe railings with benches to sit on. There they waited to be called before an inspector who would ask them twenty-nine questions. Everything depended on the answers they gave. Even though they might be prepared, there was always the fear that the all-powerful officials would find cause to send one back. Parents could be separated from children, husbands from wives. Everyone had heard of someone who had had that experience.

Chanah's family moved along a few feet of bench space at a time in a string of human beads jerking forward one by one. After what seemed like forever, they were next.

The first question was directed to Yonkel. "Who paid for your fare?" the inspector asked through an interpreter.

Yonkel straightened his collarless jacket. "I did," he replied proudly.

"Do you have a job waiting for you?"

"Yes. In Woodbine, New Jersey. I go to work on a farm."

"Is anyone meeting you?"

"No."

This answer seemed to bother the inspector, who made a note on a piece of paper.

Yonkel was next asked if he and Rifke were married. Rifke, offended, jumped up. "Of course we are married," she shouted. "What do you think we are?"

"When and where?" demanded the inspector. Rifke gave him the date and the name of the village. She would have told him more, but Yonkel gave her a warning look and she sat down, her arms angrily crossed.

"How much money do you have?"

Yonkel wanted no unexpected whacks on the head from thieves in the night. "Five dollars in gold," he whispered.

"Show it to me," demanded the inspector.

This presented a problem. Should Yonkel show his coins, which he had kept so carefully hidden, and risk losing them? Yet, without money, they were considered public charges. If the authorities decided that this was so, they would all have to wait in detention rooms from which hardly anyone was released except to be sent back to where they came from.

Yonkel reluctantly took off his shoes while the inspector and the interpreter laughed. Then each family member was asked his or her name, after which a miracle occurred. The inspector issued landing cards for all of them, including Tante Mima, whose answers were not always on the mark, especially when they asked if she knew where she was and she replied that she wasn't sure, but it was definitely not the Taj Mahal.

"Thank you," said Yonkel, using up two of his eleven English words.

Dragging their belongings, they passed through the maze of iron railings. Then they waited on the other side behind a mesh fence for Yaacov, Schmuel, and Raizel, close enough to hear what the inspector was saying to them.

Yaacov stood before the high bench in his knickers and visored hat. When the inspector asked him his name, his mother stepped forward. "He has a sore throat," she explained. "Not a sickness. Just hoarse. From calling geese. See, I have wrapped his neck in flannel."

"You've been on the ship for two weeks," said the inspector when the interpreter had relayed Raizel's answer. "As far as I know, there was not a goose among you." He laughed at his own joke.

Then things took a serious turn. The officials conferred. One stepped behind Yaacov and clapped his hands behind Yaacov's head. Chanah, who saw this coming, pointed from the fence and Yaacov turned.

"He seems to hear all right," said the interpreter.

"I'm not so sure," said the inspector. "He was slow in turning. Whisper your name, boy. Even with a sore throat, you can whisper."

"He wants your name," said the interpreter.

Yaacov drew an imaginary line down the center of his body, turned in one direction, then the other. Then he fell to the ground, rolling and threshing on the floor.

"What is he doing?" asked the inspector. "Is he having some kind of fit? If that's what he's doing, the interview is over."

Chanah broke from her family, ducked beneath the iron pipe, and ran to the high bench. "I know what he's doing. He's showing you Yaacov, in the Bible. That's his name. That's what he's saying."

"Yaacov is Jacob," explained the interpreter.

The inspector leaned over his desk to peer at Chanah. "Who are you to him?" he asked.

"He's my cousin."

"How do you know that was what he said?"

"Yaacov in the Bible was a twin. That's why he divided himself in half. And when he fell to the ground, that was Yaacov wrestling with the angel. He can talk," insisted Chanah. "He just talks with his hands. Tell him something else," she said to Yaacov.

Yaacov pointed to the inspector's pocket watch, made rippling hand motions, then a pinch of his thumb and forefinger.

"He's saying you have a drop of water inside your watchcase."

The inspector looked. Sure enough, there was a tiny drop of water under the case.

"At least we know his eyesight is good," he said.

Yonkel decided it was time to join the protest. "A different language," he shouted through the mesh. "Like all the different languages here. You need an interpreter, that's all."

Then the inspector lost his temper. "Get that little girl out of here!" he shouted. "Things are getting out of hand. Tell them to be quiet or we'll send them all back."

The inspector appeared to be troubled. He seemed to be thinking, You let in someone who's deaf, then you let in someone else who's blind. Where's it all going to end?

When the inspector shook his head, no one needed an interpreter to figure out that Yaacov would not be permitted to enter.

A great scream went up from Raizel, the kind that rattles from the throat and makes all within hearing feel their scalps crawl. Rifke began to wail, Yonkel to shout.

The interpreter, used to such scenes, explained, "The boy has to return. The mother and the other boy can stay, but this one has to go back to Poland."

Raizel began to shriek and tear at her dress, while every other mother and father in the waiting room pressed forward with their hands at their hearts, their throats, knowing that at any time, this could happen to them.

Yaacov's mother was in a painful dilemma. What to do? Her choice was simple, yet terrible: to return with Yaacov, and perhaps never see her husband, Shimson, again; worse, to let Yaacov return alone to live with distant relatives, perhaps never to see him again.

Chanah broke free from Benjamin's clutch, ducked beneath the railing, and again approached the inspector's bench. This time one of her black stockings had fallen to her high-topped shoes, but she made no move to pick it up. "He knows everything," she said. "He can tell you what you had for breakfast this morning and what you had for lunch. Ask him."

"The boy is entitled to an appeal," said the interpreter to the inspector. "You and I both know that can include the testimony of either relatives or lawyers."

"We can't afford a lawyer," shouted Yonkel.

Suddenly weary, the inspector's shoulders sagged. "All right," he said. "Tell him to tell me what I had to eat today."

Chanah asked Yaacov. Yaacov in turn made hand motions that Chanah interpreted.

"He said you had sausage and bread for lunch with coffee to drink, and eggs for breakfast."

"I'll be," said the inspector. "How did he do that?"

Chanah conferred with Yaacov. "He smells the sausage on your breath, and he sees the coffee on your teeth, the bread crumbs on your beard, and the eggs on your mustache."

The inspector cocked an eye. He reminded Chanah of a rooster that used to strut in a neighbor's yard. "How does he know that I didn't have the eggs for lunch?"

"Because the egg on your mustache is dry. If you had had it for lunch, the pieces would still be damp."

The two men looked at each other while everyone held their breath. Then the inspector winked at the interpreter. "I say we let in a kid with a sore throat." No translation was needed. The smiles told it all.

When the inspector stamped a landing permit for Yaacov, Yaacov's mother grabbed his hand and kissed it.

"Oh, now," said the inspector, "don't be making me out to be some saint." Then he became all business. "Next," he shouted, "we haven't got all day," as another family with patient, hopeful eyes came forward, bringing their belongings on their backs and their children in their arms.

♦ ♦ ♦

Chanah's family's last stop before they took the return ferry was the money exchange booth. Yonkel decided to cash only one gold coin and save the other for emergencies, which, in a family, come along at a fearsome rate. Besides, he reasoned, paper money can tear, paper money can burn, paper money can go out of fashion if one's country loses a war. But a gold coin . . . you cannot even bite into a gold coin.

Yonkel made another choice, one that cost him some of his money. A boat was available to take them directly to New Jersey, but Yonkel wanted to be sure that his cousin Shimson's family were safely met. He would take the ferry with them to New York City. It would cost him extra. A few pennies, he thought. What did it matter? If he and his entire family, including Yaacov, could make it safely through the inspection at Ellis Island, earning money would be easier than slapping a potato pancake on a griddle.

SEVEN

The family ran from the shelter of the pier to the streets and back again, looking for Shimson. If the docks of New York City were a confusion, the streets beyond were more so, with horse-drawn carriages, cable cars whirring from overhead tracks, and once in a while, when one could take one's eyes from the tops of the tall buildings, a true wonder, a horseless carriage.

Yonkel decided that they were better off waiting under the shelter of the pier. Sooner or later, Shimson would find them. Yonkel led them to the exit ramp of the ferries, where they stood rooted like trees among a horde of immigrants heading for the crowded streets.

Some were vaguely familiar. Some they knew, like the German couple who stopped to say goodbye, the father carrying the chair carved with lions, the mother proudly holding their new baby with the red ribbon pinned to her swaddling shawl.

As the waiting grew tiresome, Chanah and her family sat on their bundles until Yaacov suddenly began flicking each side of his waist and pointing excitedly to someone in the crowd.

"Look," shouted Chanah. "Yaacov is making the fringe on his father's prayer shawl!" Then Shimson appeared, excusing himself as he pushed through the crowd, looking exactly like an American. Yonkel said it was his beard, which had been shaved off. Rifke said it was more likely his suit of clothes, made of first-class American material.

"Shimson!" shouted Raizel, who had not seen her husband in two years. "Papa," shouted Schmuel, who bolted clumsily on his fat, stubby legs. Yaacov ran smiling and silent, flicking his hands at his waist.

Shimson was all good news. He had a job in the garment industry, an excellent one. He was a pants presser. In fact, he had jobs lined up for every member of his family. Raizel would sew at home while he would take the boys, both of them, to the shop, where Schmuel would sweep and Yaacov would pull threads.

"Why can't I pull threads?" complained Schmuel. "Why isn't he the one to sweep?"

Shimson paid no attention to his older son and turned to Yonkel. "Stay in New York," he advised. "With all the family working, you will be able to put aside some money."

"I don't think so," replied Yonkel. "I have made up my mind to go to New Jersey."

Rifke whispered in his ear.

"Besides," added Yonkel, "my children will go to school."

"The girl, too?" asked Shimson, with some surprise.

Yonkel wanted to say, *Especially* the girl, especially after what she did this day for your son, but such comments would make Benjamin feel unworthy. Instead he said, "Why not the girl?"

While Shimson gathered his family's belongings, assigning to each a parcel to carry, Yaacov pulled his hat over one eye and looked over his shoulder.

Chanah turned and recognized the woman from third class standing alone in the throng, like a pebble in a stream only feet from where they stood. Chanah approached the woman timidly.

"There you are," said the woman with a great sigh. "I was getting ready to let it go."

"Let what go?" asked Chanah, wondering if she meant the feather.

"See for yourself." The woman handed Chanah her blue flower-printed hatbox. Scratching sounds could be heard coming from inside.

"Go on," said the woman. "Open it."

Chanah carefully lifted the lid of the hatbox. Inside was a scrawny, tired-looking, unhappy cat. Chanah bent down, tears shining in her eyes, picked up the creature, and held her to her chest. "Pitsel. I thought I would never, never see you again," she crooned.

"And a fine mess it made of my hatbox," said the woman. "I can never use it again, I can tell you that."

Then Yonkel came shouting through the crowd. "There you are! Didn't I tell you never to leave our side? Never! Your mother is beside herself. Why would you give us such a fright?"

Chanah wiped the tears that streamed down her face. "Look, Papa," she said. "The lady kept her for me."

"What was I to do?" said the woman. "The creature followed me to my cabin. It must have been the smoked fish I had wrapped inside a napkin. Once it was inside, there was the problem of getting rid of it. I didn't want anyone to think it belonged to me. So I hid it in my hatbox, which, I might add, will never be the same."

"Thank you," said Chanah in English.

"What did she say?" asked the woman.

"She spoke English," replied Yonkel. "And she thanked you as I do. Is anyone meeting you?" he asked.

"My sister and her husband. They were supposed to be here two hours ago. I decided that as long as I was waiting for them, I would watch to see if you came out."

"If they don't show up," he said, "you are welcome to come with us to New Jersey. We are going to a farm community where there is work for all who want it and plenty of room."

"Heaven forbid," she said. "I grew up on a farm. I have no intention of going back to one, especially in a place I never heard of. Besides, I will soon have my own apartment."

Just then a woman yelled, "There she is! Looking like a greenhorn!" and a couple broke from the crowd to wrap the woman from third class in a warm embrace. The man picked up her baggage and they led her away while the woman said, "You can't sleep on the couch. Stan's cousin is sleeping there. But we made a bed for you in the kitchen."

Rifke had been standing behind Yonkel's shoulder. "No one wants to go with us to New Jersey," she said. "Maybe they know something we don't." She forgot about New Jersey when she saw the cat. Cats carried typhus, ringworm, and heaven knows what else. They were even known to suck the breath from a sleeping baby. Rifke put her hands on her hips. "No cat," she said.

Then Benjamin did something he seldom did. He put in a good word. "Cats also kill mice, Mama," he said. "And there are a lot of mice in the country."

Raizel also intervened. "Rifke, if it wasn't for Chanah, I hate to think what would have happened today."

Tante Mima had the last word. "Let the child have her cat," she said, "so we can go and I can get off my feet."

Rifke, outnumbered, gave in. "All right," she said. "But not in the house." She turned to Yonkel. "We are going to have a house, aren't we?"

"There will be a house," replied Yonkel. He did not add, Maybe not today. Neither did he say, Maybe not tomorrow. All he said was, "In this country, everything is possible."

♦ ♦ ♦

With tears and promises to write and visit, Chanah and her family said good-bye to Shimson, Raizel, Schmuel, and Yaacov and boarded the ship for New Jersey.

Chanah stood at the railing, with the basket partially opened so Pitsel could feel the sea breeze on her face. The cat, who seemed to know that all was going reasonably well, poked her head out of the basket and sniffed the salt air.

"That's some terrible-looking animal," said Rifke to Yonkel.

"I wouldn't worry," said Yonkel. "In New Jersey, you will not be able to tell her from an American cat. Mark my words."

Then Tante Mima, too weary to stand, sat on her baggage. "This is positively the last boat they'll ever get me on again. I may be an old lady, but I can still put my foot down."

"What does it mean, Bubbi," asked Chanah, "to put your foot down?"

"It means to be stubborn. It means to say yes or no and mean it. Like what you did today for your cousin. You put your foot down. And they listened." Tante Mima bent over to pull up Chanah's stocking. "Chanah, Chanah," she said, "what a little woman you are going to be."